MR.MEN **LITTLE MISS**

MR. MEN and LITTLE MISS™ © THOIP (a Chorion Company)

www.mrmen.com

Mr. Men and Little Miss™ Text and illustrations
© 2010 THOIP (a Chorion company).
Printed and published under licence from
Price Stern Sloan, Inc., Los Angeles.

Original creation by Roger Hargreaves
Illustrated by Adam Hargreaves
First published in Great Britain 1998
This edition published in Great Britain in 2010 by Dean,
an imprint of Egmont UK Limited
239 Kensington High Street, London W8 6SA

Printed in Italy
ISBN 978 0 6035 6570 0

1 3 5 7 9 10 8 6 4 2

LITTLE MISS SUNSHINE

KEEPS HER SMILE

Roger Hargreaves

DEAN

Little Miss Sunshine lives in Rise and Shine Cottage on the bank of a river.

And Little Miss Sunshine, as her name suggests, is a very happy person.

The sort of person who never gets in a bad mood.

The sort of person who is the exact opposite of somebody else who appears in this story.

That somebody is Mr Grumpy.

And Mr Grumpy, as his name suggests, is the grumpiest person in the world.

The sort of person who is always in a bad mood.

Everything annoys him.

Flowers growing in his garden. Sunny days .... and rainy days. But the thing that puts Mr Grumpy in the worst possible mood is seeing other people happy.

One morning Mr Grumpy met Little Miss Sunshine.

"Good morning Mr Grumpy," said Miss Sunshine cheerfully.

"There is nothing good about it," snapped Mr Grumpy.

"Humph," huffed Mr Grumpy, after Miss Sunshine had left. "That Miss Sunshine is always so abominably happy! Just for once I'd like to see her in a bad mood."

It was on his way home that Mr Grumpy thought of a plan. A plan to upset Little Miss Sunshine.

He raced home and made a list of all the things that were guaranteed to upset him.

It was a very long list!

"Now, there must be something here that will put Miss Sunshine in a bad mood," he said to himself.

Mr Grumpy was not a very nice man!

The first thing Mr Grumpy had written on his list was, 'waiting for buses'.

So the next day Mr Grumpy opened a gate and let all Farmer Fields' sheep out into the lane! And the bus was delayed for hours and hours while all the sheep were rounded up.

Mr Grumpy ran round to the bus stop.

"Tee hee," he chuckled nastily, "I can't wait to see how upset Miss Sunshine is."

But Little Miss Sunshine was not upset.

In fact she was not there.

It was such a nice day she had decided to walk into town.

"Bother!" said Mr Grumpy.

The next day Mr Grumpy looked at the second thing on the list.

"Losing," he read out loud.

So that evening he invited Miss Sunshine round to his house to play cards and . . . cheated!

But Little Miss Sunshine being the happy-go-lucky person she is did not mind losing.

Mr Grumpy won every game they played.

"Oh, well played Mr Grumpy," she said, at the end of the evening.

"Bother, bother," said Mr Grumpy after she had left.

Mr Grumpy read down his list again.

Number three said, 'getting caught in the rain'.

Mr Grumpy filled up his watering can and, using his ladder, climbed a tree just outside Miss Sunshine's house.

And there he waited until Miss Sunshine came out for her walk.

But Little Miss Sunshine saw
the ladder.

"What a silly place to leave a ladder,"
she said to herself, and walked round
the other side of the tree and put the
ladder away.

"Bother, bother, bother," muttered Mr Grumpy, who ended up stuck in the tree all night.

Well, nearly all night. Just before sunrise he fell asleep . . . and fell out of the tree!

The fourth thing on Mr Grumpy's list was 'queues'.

Mr Grumpy waited until Little Miss Sunshine went shopping and then he rushed ahead of her to the greengrocer's. Where he started an argument with Mrs Pod about the quality of her peas.

As he argued a queue began to grow behind him and when he glanced back he saw Miss Sunshine standing at the back of the queue.

He smiled to himself and carried on arguing until he felt sure she must be fed up of waiting.

But when he turned round the queue had disappeared and when he went outside he found everyone in the queue happily chatting with Little Miss Sunshine.

"Double bother, bother!"

Mr Grumpy was furious.

But then he met Mr Nosey and had another thoroughly nasty idea.

"Do you know," said Mr Grumpy, "what Little Miss Sunshine calls Miss Bossy behind her back? She calls her knobbly knees!"

Mr Grumpy's thoroughly nasty idea was to start a rumour that would get Little Miss Sunshine into trouble.

And the rumour spread.

Mr Nosey told Little Miss Star who told Mr Uppity who told Little Miss Splendid who told ... Mr Muddle ... who told Little Miss Bossy.

"... and Little Miss Sunshine said that Mr Grumpy calls you knobbly knees," said Mr Muddle.

"Did he now!" said Miss Bossy, grimly, and marched straight round to Mr Grumpy's house and biffed him on the nose!

It was a very sorry looking Mr Grumpy that Little Miss Sunshine met outside her house the next day.

Miss Sunshine invited him in for breakfast to cheer him up and cooked him fried eggs.

Sunny side up of course!

And did she manage to cheer up Mr Grumpy?

Of course not!

No more than Mr Grumpy can upset Little Miss Sunshine!